WITHDRAWN

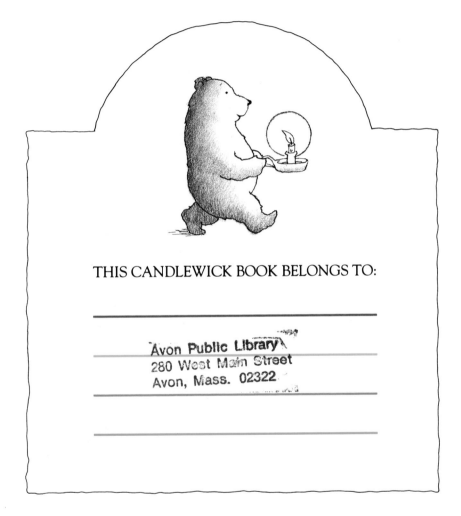

THIS CANDLEWICK BOOK BELONGS TO:

*For everyone
who loves cats,
especially
Marni*

Copyright © 1992 by Sarah Hayes

First U.S. paperback edition 1995

Library of Congress Cataloging-in-Publication Data

Hayes, Sarah.
The cats of Tiffany Street / Sarah Hayes.
Summary: When a cat catcher captures a close-knit
group of cats that likes to hang out on Tiffany Street,
Shadow the cat devises a plan to rescue them.
ISBN 1-56402-094-0 (hardcover)
ISBN 1-56402-503-9 (paperback)
[1. Cats—Fiction. 2. Stories in rhyme.] I. Title.
PZ8.3.H324Cat 1992   91-58720
[E]—dc20

2 4 6 8 10 9 7 5 3 1

Printed in Hong Kong

The pictures in this book were done in
watercolor and pencil.

Candlewick Press
2067 Massachusetts Avenue
Cambridge, Massachusetts 02140

THE CATS OF TIFFANY STREET

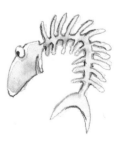

Written and illustrated by

Sarah Hayes

CANDLEWICK PRESS
CAMBRIDGE, MASSACHUSETTS

On Friday night they arranged to meet
down at the end of Tiffany Street.
They climbed out of windows,
squeezed through doors, and one
came down from the seventh floor.
There was Marmalade Ned
with his special fish head,
Captain Bligh who had only one eye,
Delicate Fan from Isfahan,
Pitter and Pat the family cats,
and Shadow the stray
who wandered all day,
searching and searching
for somewhere to stay.

Around and around to a silent beat,
they danced at the end of Tiffany Street.

Then along came the man with the van.

He snatched up Ned
and Delicate Fan

and pushed them into
the back of the van.

He snatched up Pitter.
He snatched up Pat

and Captain Bligh
the one-eyed cat.

Shadow the stray who wandered all day
quietly quietly slipped away
and hid from the man with the van.

But when the van left Tiffany Street,
Shadow was hiding under the seat.

The man in the van drove all night,
    on and on until it got light,
        when he reached an empty turkey shed . . .

and there he left poor Marmalade Ned
and Delicate Fan and Pitter and Pat
and Captain Bligh the one-eyed cat.

Shadow the stray who wandered all day
quietly quietly slipped away
and hid from the man with the van.

But when he lay down on his rollaway bed,
Shadow sang out from the roof of the shed,
"Never again will the cats all meet
to dance at the end of Tiffany Street."

And all night long she sang that song.
And all night long he heard that song
and tossed and turned on his rollaway bed
and thought with regret of the cats in the shed.
And when he couldn't take any more . . .

the man threw open the turkey-shed door.
Delicate Fan just ran and ran,
but Captain Bligh attacked the man.

Pitter and Pat hissed and spat,
and Marmalade Ned sat on his head.

Then the cats all ran away,
except for Shadow the wandering stray,
who saw that the man wasn't really bad,
just old and lonely and terribly sad.

Four months later, with very sore feet,
the cats returned to Tiffany Street.

Marmalade Ned got a new fish head.
Delicate Fan ate chicken and ham.
Pitter and Pat did this and that,
and Captain Bligh had pickerel pie.

And when they met on Tiffany Street
and danced and danced to the silent beat,
the cats all thought of that awful day
and wondered what happened to Shadow the stray.

Shadow was far from Tiffany Street,
in a place she had found with plenty to eat
and a home and a lap and a rollaway bed,
with the man in the van and the turkey shed.

SARAH HAYES adores cats and wrote this book after there was "a terrible spell of cats being snatched in my area and I began to wonder about the kind of person who would take a cat." She based the heroine of her story, Shadow, on her own gray cat. Sarah Hayes is also the author of *This Is the Bear* and the reteller for *The Candlewick Book of Fairy Tales*.